I Like to Read® books, created by award-winning
picture book artists as well as talented newcomers,
instill confidence and the joy of reading in new readers.

We want to hear every new reader say, "I like to read!"

_____

Visit our website for flash cards, activities, and more about the series:
www.holidayhouse.com/ILiketoRead
#ILTR
This book has been tested by an educational expert
and determined to be a guided reading level B.

I Like
My Car

Michael Robertson

I Like to Read®

HOLIDAY HOUSE • NEW YORK

HOLIDAY HOUSE is registered in the U.S. Patent and Trademark Office.

Printed and Bound in April 2018 at Tien Wah Press, Johor Bahru, Johor, Malaysia.

The artwork was created with water-based printing inks, an etching press, an onion bag, and digital tools.

www.holidayhouse.com

First Edition

1 3 5 7 9 10 8 6 4 2

Library of Congress Cataloging-in-Publication Data is available.

ISBN 978-0-8234-3951-5 (hardcover)

ISBN 978-0-8234-3952-2 (paperback)

To my mother, Carmelinda,
who always steered me in the right direction
even though I sometimes drove her crazy.

I like my red car.

I like my blue car.

I like my yellow car.

I like my pink car.

I like my purple car.

I like my green car.

I like my green car too.

I like my black car.

I like my white car.

I like my car.